For Françoise who said, "Why don't you
do a book about football called Goal!?"
And I said "Hmm ..."

First published in Great Britain in 1997 by Andersen Press Ltd., 20 Vauxhall
Bridge Road, London SW1V 2SA. This paperback edition first published in
2016 by Andersen Press Ltd.
Copyright © 1997 Colin McNaughton
The rights of Colin McNaughton to be identified as the author and illustrator
of this work have been asserted by him in accordance with the Copyright,
Designs and Patents Act, 1988.
All rights reserved.
Colour separated in Italy by Fotoriproduzioni Beverari, Verona.
Printed and bound in China.

10   9   8   7   6   5   4   3   2   1

British Library Cataloguing in Publication Data available.

ISBN 978 1 78344 554 7

Goal!

Words and Pictures by
Colin McNaughton

Andersen Press
London

Preston is playing football
in the garden one day,

A loaf
of bread,
please,
pumpkin.

when his mum asks him
to go to the shop. Preston
decides to take his ball

and Preston, the world's most brilliant footballer, sets off.

He beats one player, then
another, goes round the
goalkeeper and shoots...

And the fans go wild:
"Ooh-ah-Preston Pig.
I said ooh-ah-Preston Pig!"

And Preston has the ball once more. He runs the whole length of the park and shoots…

It's a

goal!

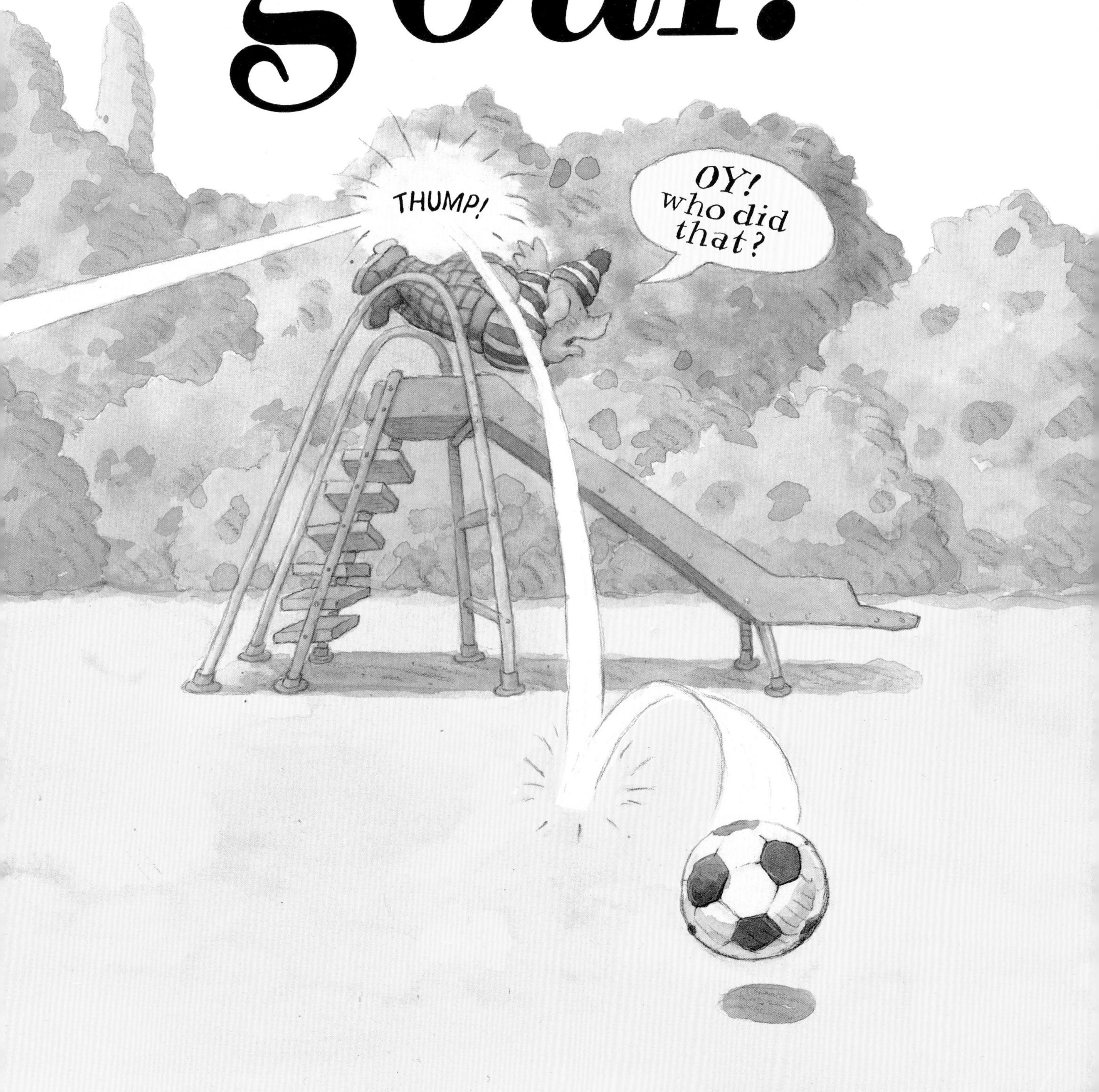

And the huge crowd chants:
"Preston, Preston,
He's the best 'un!"

And Preston goes looking
for his hat-trick.

And this is incredible!
He's off on another run!
He goes round one. He goes
round two, three and he shoots...

That makes it three goals to nil,

He dribbles past the great Pele, swerves past the magical Maradona,

sweeps past Shearer,
puts the ball through the
legs of Cantona and shoots…

Four goal Preston sets off
home with the bread.

Mister Wolf leaves
the supermarket.

Mister Wolf takes a shortcut
and lies in wait for Preston.

And Mister Wolf
gobbles Preston up.

Well, not really,
but that was his plan.

Extra time